DATING blind

AMY OLIVEIRA

This is a work of fiction. Names, characters, places, and incidents either are the product of the author's imagination or are used fictitiously. Any resemblance to actual persons, living or dead, events, or locales is entirely coincidental.

Copyright © 2021 by Amy Oliveira

All rights reserved. No part of this book may be reproduced or used in any manner without written permission of the copyright owner except for the use of quotations in a book review. For more information, address: amyoliveira.com

First e-book edition February 2021

Ilustration by Ilustratam
Edited by Blazing Butterfly Edits

ISBN: *9798719850023*

www.amyoliveira.com

to all the romantics out there

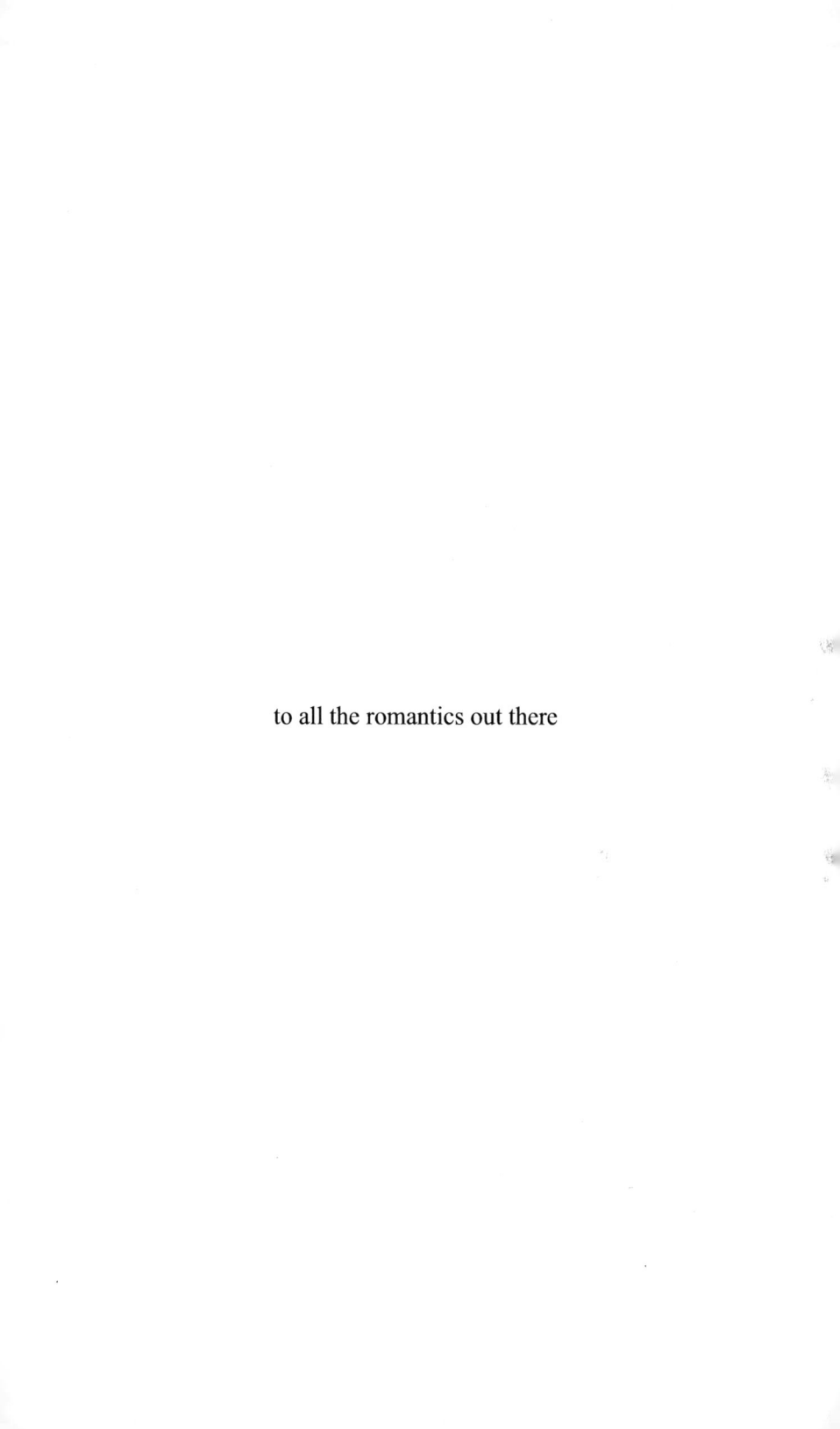

Love is patient, **love** is kind. It does not envy, it does not boast, it is not proud. It is not rude, it is not self-seeking, it is not easily angered, it keeps no record of wrongs. **Love** does not delight in evil but rejoices with the truth.

WNB announces the release date for its new Dating Reality Show!

WNB executives are excited for the new format and believe it will be a hit with the viewers.

Scheduled to air its first episode on Valentine's Day, **Dating Blind** was created and based on the theories and social experiments of the famous Dr Bernard, author of the celebrated bestseller, **Love has Changed**.

We got a hold of Dr Bernard and she shared, with our reporter Juliet Higgs, a few insights of her research and what to expect from WNB's new show.

Juliet: Thank you very much for agreeing to talk to us, Dr Bernard.

Dr Bernard: My pleasure.

Juliet: Let's start with your research and all that you've been working. Can you explain on layman's terms to our readers?

Dr Bernard: Of course. We all know how women's health had been ignored for many decades. When we take the birth control pill which was a complete revolution, still to this day, the generally agreed upon criteria is the continued use by women in trial, but those women don't represent the reality of the entire *population. The assumption for distribution IS healthy, straight sized women.*

Juliet: So, you're telling me the biggest medication that has been prescribed to all women, even before being sexually active, it might not be the best for everyone?

Dr Bernard: One size does never fit all. That's just one example how science has been in servitude to a sample human who, in reality, does not exist.

Juliet: I didn't know that!

Dr Bernard (with a smile): Not everyone knows it. That's why we need more women in science.

Juliet: Amazing. So, with this knowledge you decided to turn your research to sexuality?

Dr Bernard: Initially yes. I knew whatever we knew about women's sexuality was erroneous and dated. For a start, I wanted to focus in that.

Juliet: Did your focus change?

Dr Bernard: Oh yes. Once I started diving in, I noticed the notion of sexuality has been changed across all genders. Not just that we understand gender differently but many people say they will be open to a relationship with anyone as long as they shared the same values.

Juliet: Was that a surprise to you?

Dr Bernard: A little. Of course I knew our understanding as people had evolved, but it was surprising to see the data right in front of me.

Juliet: And that's when you started to focus more on relationships than sexuality?

Dr Bernard: Previous data shows the subjects were always classified before answering the questions. Social studies were published telling us the most important thing to the population was "religion," "money," but once you pre-group the people according to their sexual preference, you cut the data in half.

DATING BLIND

Juliet: So you think most people's preference can be wrong?

Dr Bernard: No. I believe is the 21st century, the world has many variants. People have different priorities; other factors are more important than a sexual organ. Especially since not every man has a penis, and not every woman menstruates.

Juliet: That's true. But also, that was always the case.

Dr Bernard: At least my mother hadn't grew up with that notion. She never stopped to think if she felt attracted to the penis, to the male form or if she was attracted to any man whatsoever. She married young and was assumed she wanted to marry a cis man. Now we know better than that. We know gender is a social construct and sexuality is a spectrum. More than that, people are open to meet and date someone, regardless of their gender.

Juliet: You said people find other things more important to look in a partner than sex organs? Can you give us an example?

Dr Bernard: Politics for a start.

Juliet: I was going to guess that!

Dr Bernard: Definitely. Political alignment is most people's number one. Other things as well, like the type of life they want to live, values and morals. Children is a big one. It might seem like the children conversation was always around, but for long time a woman was so pressured to be a mother that many couples ignored the conversation entirely because it was a given. Now people are talking about it in the early days; women are not ashamed to say if they don't wish to be mothers.

Juliet: So, can you tell us how that relates to WNB's new show?

Dr Bernard: Dating Blind is a dating show like many before. People who are in search for the one who applied. But instead of stating their preferred gender, they told us what they are looking in a partner, emotionally speaking.

Juliet: It can be argued that it was done before. Other dating shows had people ignore the physical attributes to fall in love.

Dr Bernard: When you take gender out of the conversation it creates a range of possibilities. Those shows were always a place of good-looking cis people, because gender and sexuality was the first criteria. They said you fall in love with the person, but in reality, you fall in love with a penis or a vagina first.

Juliet: I guess that's true.

Dr Bernard: Dating Blind is for people who want to find someone to share a life with. People who believe the same things they believe and want to build a life the same way they want. Gender is the last thing on our minds when we talk about love.

WNB's Dating Blind season premiere this Sunday at 9pm.

Producer: *Can you say your name, age and where you're from to the camera?*

My mother always says not to fidget. It is unbecoming of a young lady like myself. Perhaps that's why I fidget so much, because I was told many times not to do it. Honestly, it wasn't the only thing I was told not to do. From the age of five, I only have memories of the countless things I did which frustrated my mother.

I would say it's exhausting, but she says to never show tiredness.

I know the producer can tell I'm very nervous, I have never been in front of a camera before and right now I have two big ones pointing directly at me.

The producer talking to me is named Kelly. She seems nice, has a low sweet voice, but I notice the way she looks at the crew; she's the boss.

"Gianna Miriam McKenna, I'm twenty-seven years old, from

Oldmill."

Kelly laughs. "Now say it like you aren't terrified."

I catch her looking to my fidgeting hands and I stop immediately.

"Just look at me, try to forget the cameras," Kelly says.

"It's hard," I squeak.

Kelly doesn't say it, but it's right on my mind what we are all thinking: I had signed up for this. No one made me do it, no friend had pressured me. Actually, just Maria knows what I am doing this morning.

I saw the casting call randomly one night and I thought Dr Bernard's theories and research were interesting and probably true. I was old enough to go on many dates through the years, blind ones and not, and all of them failed. It was clear I needed someone who shared the same world view than I had, who wanted to live life like I'd plan to live.

It was a great idea, I'm still certain it is, but when I responded with my questionnaire, I never really took the cameras in consideration. I let myself get seduced by the research part of things and completely forgot about the producers and the lights.

Right from the second I arrived, when I was called to make-up and someone had a good look at my body and suggested a change of clothes, I knew I was in deep trouble. I wasn't easy-going, I wasn't going to flourish in front of the camera.

I look over at Kelly and she gives an encouraging smile so I try again, "I'm Gianna Miriam McKenna from Oldmill and I'm twenty-seven years old."

I smile scared and Kelly smiles in return, "Much better. Can you talk a little about yourself?"

I nod. "I'm a volunteer in a hospital, I like colouring books…" and I blush a little. "I don't know, is that lame?"

Kelly shakes her head. "And what would be your perfect date?"

"I'd have to say April 25th. Because it's not too hot and not too cold. All you need is a light jacket," and I of course, chuckle like a loser. "Sorry, my perfect date would be anything and anywhere with whoever got that reference."

Kelly's eyebrow shoots up and she looks to the camera to her right side. "That's good, Gianna. You're TV gold."

I pass my hands over my face forgetting, for a second, about the heavy make-up I have on, "I find that hard to believe. Is it looking too dorky?"

"In an adorable way," Kelly guarantees. "Let's go over that one more time, and do you want to add anything? Something about looking for love or ready to settle down?"

I shake my head emphatically. "God no, I said already too much. Will my date see this?"

"No, this is just for the show. The audience will know you all first and then see the interaction between you two. We are the only ones in the know." She winked at me, like it was something to be excited about.

I shuffle in my seat, telling myself to calm down. While I don't want to state it to the camera, I do want to find someone to be with. Probably because I watched too many romantic comedies this Christmas, but suddenly this urge to share my life with someone came over me. This intense need to have a person right on my corner.

Kelly goes over what we talked about once more. I understand why they do it. I know my voice sounds less shaky and I have an easy smile in place. Once it's said it's out there, you can't take back. They will air it regardless, so I try to give them a little more. A better take than my awkward smile.

"And Gianna," Kelly says looking down at her notes, "Just so we have it here, what kind of person are you used to going out with? Is there any chance of you giving up on dating by gender?"

It's such an unusual way to put it, but I don't miss the uncomfortable scratch she gives to her right cheek. I look right at her, and from her to the small patch of hair on camera man number one and the small bald spot on camera man number two.

Dr Bernard's research might be ground-breaking, but a reality show is a reality show. They want to have me on camera telling how many times I had a bad date with a man, the worse the better.

I bite the insides of my cheeks and think of a diplomatic answer. I'm my mother's daughter after all.

Slowly I shake my head. "I have never dated much. I didn't

give up on anything. I simply think Dr Bernard's findings are interesting and worth a shot. I would even go ahead and say they are… freeing."

"You feel free to date any person you'd like."

It was a clever way to put it, to stir me back the way they wanted to have me.

"Free to see what's important."

Producer: *Gianna, through this door here, please.*

I'm not sure in what order things will come out. That's something I know: editing is a mosaic that is put together in the most entertaining way. I promised myself to keep this interesting. Praying about over-editing is not necessary.

Part of me fears the reality show business, and the other part is being seduced little by little.

They put us in a hotel and transport is provided all mornings. I had been in the lift twice since starting, and I always catch myself looking side to side, imagining who could be part of the show as well. But it's easy to notice they are careful; if I ever share the lift with anyone, they are always older couples or hotel staff.

This morning the last hairdresser who fixed my hair isn't around. I'm given the snippy one instead. He doesn't need to say much, just by his face I know he thinks highly of himself and very low of me. He calls my hair dry within the first three minutes we are together. But says most curly hair is, so I'm not to take it too personally. He looked me over in the mirror, eyes like a slit staring at my thick, ginger, curly hair, as he takes offense.

Finally, makeup arrives and I'm told the most flattering things. I smile since, at least, for this morning my self-esteem depends on it. She's adamant that my big blue eyes are the most gorgeous she has ever seen. They fail to understand I'm not really getting ready for a date though. No one is going to see me in the beautiful makeup and the smooth hair after a glorious blow dry. Well, no one but the cameras and probably a million people at their homes.

After I'm ready, I have to wait for my turn in a room with nine more people; I counted. I survey the place and the characters who are with me on this journey. As Dr Bernard promised, they all look genuine and I'm grateful for that. No one carries any defining characteristics. I don't know how to judge them based on if they got tea or coffee. I wait once more, my feet hopping up and down, trying not to rub my face and ruin the makeup.

The room is all grey, boring walls and white cheap furniture. Piles of old magazines lay on a little flimsy Ikea table. I get myself a cup of tea and end up biting the rim of the cup once I finish.

It's useless, I'm nervous.

There are two doors on the right, apart from the door we all came in. I assume it leads to the studios, and I find I'm correct when the first two people are called separately to film and they disappear through the doors.

Twenty minutes later, when two more people are called in, I see Kelly coming into the room and she shoots me a smile; my spine stands straight right away.

"Nervous?" The man beside me asks with a wavery smile.

I nod. "I don't know if I like to be on camera."

Another uncertain smile, "I'm Jeff."

"Gianna."

Jeff looks like a normal guy, wearing a plain t-shirt, old jeans, a battered cap and has a gentle face.

"I'm more nervous about the date. If they are going to like me."

I frown. "I thought that was the point. They are going to select someone who likes the same things as me, so why wouldn't they like me?"

Jeff shrugs. "I don't know. I don't think that's exactly how we work, or we would be in relationship with all our friends, uh?"

I bite my lip and lose myself in thought. He's right, there has to be more to the recipe, something extra to spice up the love. It just never occurred to me what could be, I never thought maybe I didn't have it.

"Don't worry," Jeff says. "You look like a nice girl, people will probably like you."

"I think people like me." I frown again. "They just don't seem to like me like me."

DATING BLIND

"That's the reason why we are all here, isn't it? If we had people that loved us why would we be looking for someone on TV?"

My stomach churns. "I was not made for TV, I get too nervous. I'm probably not likable on screen."

"I'm sorry, did I freak you out?"

I chuckle anxiously. "No, it wasn't you Jeff. I was nervous before." I smile at him. "I'm sure they will like you too."

Jeff takes his cap and sinks it further onto his head in an obvious attempt to pretend he isn't flattered.

Kelly's voice interrupts our talk. She asks me to go through the door. I follow her request, smiling at the companion I'd left behind.

The room looks beautiful, but I know it's just a set. The comfortable-looking white chair is right in the middle with a shaggy rug underneath, and a glass table with a white laptop with a *Dating Blind* logo sticker on top. The set walls are blinding white with big geometric patterns and golden lines.

"You can sit right there, Gianna," Kelly encourages me.

I nod and hurry myself to sit, my legs feel a bit wobbly. It's the set effect, the cameras and lights point at me and all of a sudden is like I can't breathe.

"Tea, coffee, a can of coke?"

"Something stronger?" I joke.

"Beer, vodka or whiskey?" Kelly says without missing a beat.

God, the last thing I need is to get drunk on TV, but of course it's what they want. So, I just shake my head and sink further in the chair. "Just a cup of tea, please."

A different make-up artist fusses over me while they are adjusting cameras, lights and whatnots. I have no idea what they are doing, I just watch everything while trying to calm my nerves.

Some kid with a pimpled face who I could swear was still in school comes over and places the tea in front of me. I smile in gratitude but he hurries away. Kelly is talking fast with a tall guy, they come in my direction even though they don't seem to pay attention.

"Gary will get you ready, ok?"

I barely nodded and Gary is wiring a microphone on me, sticking stuff through my back and placing a device on my jeans.

"Today is really simple Gianna," Kelly says fast. "You have twenty minutes to have your first contact to your chosen match. We like you to keep it light this time around. No serious conversations, no exchange of information of any kind, alright?"

"What will we talk about?"

"Start with a silly opener," she advises. "You know, maybe something about that film you'd mentioned?"

I shake my head straight away. "No, I don't think *Miss Congeniality*..."

"Kelly!" someone calls in the background and she moves away from me.

I'm left alone as I watch them all around me, telling each other things that I have no idea what it means. I pick up my tea with shaky hands and bring it to my mouth. I try my best to use my other hand to stabilise the shakes but it doesn't make much difference.

The same pimpled intern comes around and turns on the laptop placed on the table, but he doesn't say a word to me. More than a couple of minutes pass and I'm still confused about what I am supposed to be doing, but each time I open my mouth to ask, I end up closing it again.

"Is your computer set, Gianna?" Kelly asks me.

I take a second to answer, I have no idea what she means by "set." Yes there is a computer in front of me, yes it is on, but that's as far as I can tell. The second wait is too much for Kelly anyway so she comes to me and bends over the computer, "Did anyone explain what we are about to do?"

I shake my head, the only thing I know is what she just told me. She turns to me for a second and back to the computer. "This is how you are talking to your match, uh? We blow up your messages and all after?"

She turns to me again and I nod, I don't know exactly what she's saying but I find it better to agree right away.

"Here." Kelly steps away and shows it to me.

On the screen is a simple white and gold text box, and the computer has the show's logo as a screensaver.

Kelly texts something in the text box and shows it to me. "See? No names?" She's right, my message is sent and appears in the top box in purple letters but no name comes with it.

Kelly steps away without saying anything else, I know I need to ask more but I'm still staring at the message box.

"Is everyone ready?" Kelly asks to the whole crew. I look to her and she asks directly to me this time, "Ready?"

I see they are turning the cameras to me. I frown, prepared to ask what is next, but the ping on the computer distracts me. In red letters it says:

"Hello."

"Welcome to Dating Blind!"

Melanie Steward, model and TV host, walks in clouds around the white and gold set of Dating Blind. Her beaming smile is contagious, the clothes pristine and perfect.

"Welcome to Dating Blind, the dating show where the way you look..." a dramatic pause and a smile. "Is not important at all."

"Our thirty-two hopefuls initially are going to be online chatting with their perfect match. On the next round only the couples who want to meet will remain."

Photos of the contestants fill the screen, one by one, until there's a mosaic of thirty-two smiling people. WNB promised real people and they deliver. The Dating Blind cast isn't just a bunch of models.

The image is back to Melanie Steward and the Dating Blind logo to her left side. "Ready to meet our heroes?"

The screen changes for the pre-recorded interviews. The first is Nadia, 37. With her long chocolate hair resting on her left shoulder and a white blouse, she shuffles on the seat, but has a firm smile on her lips.

"Oh yes I'm nervous. It's hardly an everyday event," Nadia says. "I'm Nadia, I'm a doctor... head physician to be fair..." she tries a modest smile, but ends up shaking her head.

Nadia rubs her hands together and stares at the camera. "I've been preoccupied with my career, I admit. We always think there's time until..." she shrugs and give a little nervous smile.

Nadia is gone, a man in a ball cap replaces her. He scratches his cheek and shakes his head with a shy smile. It says: Jeff, 34.

"Sometimes we go to one, two, even three dates and you have an alright time, isn't it? Then you realise you've been dating a racist this whole time?" Jeff chuckles and shakes his head again, "No one starts a conversation telling you all the shitty things they believe, I reckon they know is shitty, uh? So they keep it until the last minute and bam! What a waste of a month."

Josh, 23 is on the screen. He's a good looking man, with thick black hair, he's sitting on his wheelchair and smiling confidently.

"I just think it's easy if you know everything about them, am I right?" He says and shrugs, "I blocked family members of my social media accounts due political differences, I don't know why would I accept any less from people I date."

Once more the screen changes, it reads Natalie, 42 on the bottom. A blond woman with pink undertones on her skin and a bright smile.

"My ex-husband used to say all these things as a joke, and I thought it were a joke..." Natalie pauses and her smile almost slips away, "I don't think they were jokes anymore. We got married young, no one used to ask the important questions twenty years ago" She nods to herself, "I know so much about myself, I had to learn the hard way how strong I am and the things I won't admit to be said to me," she smiles, "I think I'm ready."

It's the turn of Trevor, 25. He has an easy smile, a shaved head and dark skin, Trevor rubs his hands together in excitement.

"Wouldn't you be ready? If someone promised you they have a way to find your perfect match? Wouldn't be your favourite day?" Trevor's smile get bigger, "Listen, who cares. If they tell me this is the person who will bring happiness for your life until the end of days. A girl, a bloke, whoever. You can't start happily ever after soon enough!"

Trevor's excited smile fades on screen and Gianna comes along. It reads Gianna, 27 and she's biting her lip, looking a little nervous.

"I have never dated much. I didn't gave up on anything, I simply think Dr Bernard's findings are interesting and worth a shot. I would even go ahead and say they are… freeing. Free to see what's important."

Melanie Steward is back on the studio, the same good natured smile plastered on her rose lips.

"Today they will be having the first conversation with their perfect match. They don't know anything about each other: gender, social economic status, physical attributes. It's a complete blind date. Our first couple are waiting. Let's have a look?"

Producer: *Reply, Gianna!*

Kelly's rushed whisper wakes me up. I look at her, and she nods towards the computer, I look back in front of me. I place my hand on the keyboard and stare at those five red letters.

"Hi," I write back in purple.

"Oh, hi... You took your time," they reply.

"I'm sorry, they are pointing those cameras at me. It makes me so nervous."

"I know..." the red letters' answer makes me relax a little. It's good to share it with someone who gets it.

"They said we have to talk about something light and easy..." I type.

"They pair up people who believe in morals and values more than status and gender and expect we have a light conversation," red types.

I giggle instantaneously and of course it's a good sign, if wasn't the camera man quickly approaching, I would had forgotten I was still on set.

"You made me laugh and the cameras went ballistic," I tell them.

"Sorry for that. I will try my best not to be entertaining. Tell me, what's your favourite vegetable?"

I hold my mouth not to laugh. "I'm weirdly passionate about broccoli."

"Of all the vegetables... I'm allergic."

I can't hold and I free laugh this time. "No, you're not."

"Cross my heart hope to die..."

"Is this whole thing a hoax? Wouldn't they know we aren't the perfect match if I love broccoli and you are allergic to it?"

"One can hope you'll protect me from the evil broccoli."

"Will I eat my way to your heart?"

"Reaching..."

I chuckle and throw my head up, I turn and see Kelly's excited expression, she's looking to the monitor of a computer instead of what is being filmed. Of course they are reading everything we are saying. How else could they make a show with people talking online?

She mouths out *Miss Congeniality* to me and I roll my eyes.

"Did you say something stupid during your interviews?"

The reply comes quickly, "Something I wished I haven't said?"

"Yes, kind of."

I can see they are typing, but it takes a second this time, "Not specifically. What do you wish you haven't said?"

"I made a stupid joke with a line from *Miss Congeniality*. And now it's like a big thing." I write.

"The 25th of April?" Comes straight away.

I shake my head with a silly smile on my lips, "Yes."

"It's a good joke."

"I don't want all my conversations to go around *Miss Congeniality* though."

"Are they trying to get you talk to me about it?"

"Yes."

"They are out of luck, I watched it just once, when it came out, but I had a cousin who was obsessed about it and they post that quote every 25th of April."

"I do too," I confess.

"Maybe you both are soulmates…"

I laugh again, this is the easiest conversation I had ever had. "Calm your horses, this is not about soulmates, uh? It's a perfect match."

"What's the difference?" red replies.

I take a second to think, eventually I say, "Isn't soulmates something cosmic, past lives and all that? Perfect match is more like a choice. Who we are right now makes us good together. Our daily choices and our beliefs."

"I like the sound of perfect match better."

"Me too."

I know it's going well. I'm not sure if my conversation is television worthy, but I know whoever had us matched had it absolutely right.

I see Kelly whispering to a camera man. They move behind me to get an over the shoulder shot, I try my best to block their movements. I have to pay attention only to the computer if I want to really connect with this person behind the screen.

I want to ask them what made them sign up for the show, what they think of the research and if they read about it in its entirety, like myself. Nothing of such is allowed though, they want to us keep it light and I didn't think was going to be so hard, but obviously once I have a nice rhythm going it's hard not to wish I could ask about anything.

Red types again, "We covered vegetables and world celebrated films, what else is there to talk about?"

"Everything that comes to mind might be too deep, it's hard to keep it meaningless."

"Light is hardly meaningless, but I like that you equate both. What about books? What's the last book you read?"

I don't want to admit it, but I end up typing anyway, "I'm terrible at choosing books, I end up getting any nonsense on the best sellers shelf."

"Me too. I'm usually reading technical books from my profession... Profession that I'm told to keep a secret..."

"I can't wait to find out. Can I get a clue?"

"No way, they will kick me out of the program if I say more."

"Now I'm almost certain you're a spy."

"Maybe... maybe... Are you a spy?"

"Ask me the secret spy password."

I wait, biting my lip for the reply but the text box disappear and I frown in confusion.

"That was great, Gianna!" Kelly says happily.

I'm still confused, wondering why they are gone. I have no idea how long were we talking, but the whole crew seems to be moving along. Kelly comes to me with a big smile. "That was great. I could feel the chemistry between you two!"

"Could be better if you hadn't cut my conversation..."

But Kelly is shaking her head and walking back, wagging her finger at me she says, "Amazing, Gianna, great work."

Producer: *Nervous?*

It's not Kelly looking at me this time around, which is odd. Since the start of filming of *Dating Blind,* I had never met another producer or anyone who was higher on the hierarchy than Kelly. Of course I knew she wasn't the show runner or anything like that, but everyone in set seemed to trust her opinions and respect her directions.

Sitting in the white chair, I knew it was interview day. I'm back in the same clothes they put me on for the first interview. It never occurred to me I would be talking to someone other than Kelly, and when it comes to our little confessions her work is almost like a therapist. One who really forces their way into a breakthrough.

Nevertheless, they had never guaranteed I would only have Kelly as my producer, so the man before me had to do.

"I'm not as nervous as the first day no..."

He nods. He doesn't really look at me, his face is down looking at his phone. "How'd you find the first connection?"

"I liked it a lot," I confirmed. "They are fun and easy to talk to."

"Yeah… yeah…" He's distracted and puts me off straight away.

I look around at the camera man to the rest of the crew and the main jerk in front of me. I know he wants interesting, television worthy answers but I can't give them if he doesn't give something, too. How can I be witty talking to a door?

"You look uncomfortable," he says. "Are you afraid the person you've been chatting is someone of a different gender that you are used to date?"

"No, *you* are making me uncomfortable."

Everyone stands still, the silence breathes around us. I worked with an asshole before. I watched for months and months as he mistreated the hospital's staff and every patient who came his way. I remember feeling impotent, as if nothing I did mattered, like I was too small and insignificant to fight back. I was shy and young and I would have never thought my threats would be enough to remove him.

A small-town lawyer decided to take action against him. The nursing staff was scared to come forward and lose their jobs, but I was a volunteer. I lived, and still live, off my family's money. Suddenly I knew if anyone was able to stop and testify against him, that would be me. If they threated to remove me, if I could never go back to the hospital, it was alright.

In the end nothing of such happened, our lawyer pressured

the board and told them I could testify if necessary. The board was too scared of a scandal and removed Dr Abram from Oldmill Memorial. I wished for a better resolution. I hoped he would not be allowed to practice medicine altogether or at least something more dramatic than a transfer. However, that's what we got.

Since Dr Abram, I had forced myself to talk back, fight back. I was still the same shy little Gianna, I wasn't going to raise my voice more than necessary, but I had to learn I mattered, the hard way.

The new producer arches his eyebrows and sits back with a smirk. I continue, "If you want a good segment you have to give me good questions."

"Thanks for teaching how to do my job, love…"

I sigh, I'm not in the mood to have to deal with him, I'm supposed to be all happy and talking about how great the first contact was with my match.

"Gianna, can you tell us a little bit how you felt with the first chat?"

I'm watching the jerk, but that question doesn't come from him. My head turns to the left when one of the camera men spoke. The rude producer shoots daggers with his eyes, but I'm quick enough to answer and cut down his rage.

"I felt hopeful. As first dates go, it was definitely one of my best."

"Did you feel it was a bit odd? Doing it online?" The question comes from the back, I lift my neck to see over the people around and the crew turns to see the makeup artist closer to the back door.

"We all had done a little of online dating, didn't we?" I chuckle. "It felt better than swiping through faces and more faces. Being on the show was already a common ground."

"What did you learn about their personality from that only interaction?" That question came from the pimpled intern, it made me open a big smile at him.

"I'd learned they have a great sense of humour, which is very important to me. In a very witty kind of way, sarcastic. Maybe they're British." The crew laughs and I laugh with them.

I try my best not to look at the jerk producer again. I'm simply not in the mood to see his sour face. I heard only a couple of sentences from him and I already can tell he isn't dedicated to the experiment. So, I try not care about him the same way he looks bored and annoyed about my dating life.

"Gianna, are you excited for the next date?" the intern asks me.

I nod and a little giggle comes out. "I can't wait, actually."

When the filming is finished, the jerk producer leaves his chair at once and slams the door behind him. No one seems very concerned though, no one goes to see if he's ok.

"He's…" one of the camera men say to me, and he rolls his eyes, "He's something…"

I stand up while being helped by a couple of people trying to take the mic off me. "What's your name?"

"I'm Michael?" he almost sounds uncertain of his own name.

"Thanks for the help, Michael. It's already awkward enough to chat about my dating life without having to deal with... well," and I whisper the next part, "with an asshole on the set."

"Kelly will be back tomorrow, she just took a personal day," he tells me.

I breathe easy. "Thank god."

"Don't you agree?"

I look around at the usual people in the waiting room. Jeff is certain they would never leave our match in the same waiting room as us. He said this before, and I have to agree, that sounds like a reasonable precaution, now one participant is missing and Jeff thinks that's the proof he needs.

"Maybe they are sick today," I whisper to him.

"Nah," he shakes his head. "We had the first contact. Maybe someone didn't like it."

I frown and mindlessly bite the rim of the plastic cup in my hands once more. "We had one contact. What is there not to like?"

Jeff shrugs. "What is there to like? We don't know anything about them."

I bite my lip not sure. "I had a great first impression."

"Me too!" He smiles big.

"See…" I nudge him with my elbow, "They chose our perfect matches! Why someone would give away…"

"You're thinking that in a weird light." The voice comes from my right side.

He approaches in a wheelchair, fixing his hair while he talks.

"What you have to remember are the cameras," he says and stops just in front of our chairs. "I'm Josh."

I see what Josh means. Still, for some reason it's hard to imagine someone would leave the program so soon in the game.

"And since we are separated so we don't meet our matches," says Jeff, "today there's a person missing here, and in another waiting room as well."

Josh points to Jeff. "That makes sense," and he looks at me. "Right?"

I shrug. "Yeah, but I would like to think people are taking this seriously."

"They are!" says Jeff at the same time Josh says, "Who cares…"

"I care! Don't you? Imagine how horrible it is thinking you're doing so well with someone just to find out the next day they decided to leave? That's horrifying."

"We clearly have very different notions of horrifying." Josh chuckles.

"I'm probably not your match." I shoot at him.

Jeff laughs and I shake my head. "I'm just trying to forget about the cameras for a second and see it in a more of a romantic light maybe?"

"I still think is romantic," Jeff tells us with his usual calming voice. "Yes, it's an experiment and not everyone will stay until the end. You guys remember what they told us on our first day?"

We both nod. I had read in the contract before, but they still reminded us on the same day we arrived at the hotel. If we decided to move along from the show it can only be done between phases and we have to give a final interview. Jeff was right, even the network was counting on having a few people give up.

"And think about it," Josh adds. "They can't keep a full season following so many couples, can they? I think they were already imagining it will thin out."

Josh is, again, speaking the truth, that would make much better TV after all. Thinning the participants out would help the audience have a better connection to the remaining ones. And yet, I wasn't comfortable to admit that maybe this whole thing had a script.

"You're scaring her," Jeff told Josh.

I shake my head. "No, it's ok. You are both right."

"I'm sure your match is taking it seriously, Gianna," Jeff assures me anyway. "I'm sure they are, alright?"

I nod in agreement because I'm grateful for Jeff, if anything.

"We are ready for you, Josh," says one of the producers from the door and Josh nods.

"At least we know my match stayed, uh?" he says back to us and then follows the producer in.

Producer: *Let's start, Gianna.*

I nod to Kelly, the *Dating Blind* logo staring at me from the laptop screen. The fact that it looks like a normal laptop feels odd, and I'm just sitting on a chair typing to someone. Of course I have two cameras watching me while I do so, but it makes me almost feel at home.

"Are you there or have you given up?"

The red letters flash on the screen and I open a smile.

"I could be anyone really."

"Let me rephrase it then, is this the *Miss Congeniality* lover?"

I actually laugh out loud. "I'm not that bad. It was one joke…"

"And that's how you shall be remembered."

"What a horrible fate!" I gasped out loud and I knew Kelly was jumping up and down of happiness.

The red letters come up again and I wish to know if they are laughing like I was. "You know what they have for us today?"

I look in front of me on the table, is a phone. Not my phone, just a black iPhone sitting there, the ping makes me look back to the screen, "Quizzes."

I see on the side Kelly signalling for me to get the phone, and I do so, it's unlocked with only the internet browser app. I open and it has Buzzfeed quizzes open. I can't stop my laugh.

"What do you reckon?" they ask.

"How much can we learn from each other by just taking this kind of quiz?" I type.

"I think the point might be just to let it go and have fun together? I once went to a wedding and they had those kinds of fun questions for the guests at each table."

"Define fun."

"It was pretty mediocre, but I get the thought."

"Let's do the soup one?" I type.

I hope they think it's humours. It's a silly quiz that we have to rate soups in order to figure out our vibe. It was definitely the most stupid of the lot and that's what made me want to take it.

"I hate all soups, let's do this," says the reply.

I barely open it and a message comes, "I hate chicken noodle soup."

I laugh out loud again, it's the first soup we have to rate. I give it a "Yum", and reply, "I love it. It's the ultimate comfort food."

"If I'm feeling sick, I'll have a couple of paracetamols and a nice carb-filled meal."

"I wouldn't say no to a nice carbonara."

I look down at the phone once more and I can't stop my laugh, there's a picture of a broccoli cheddar soup.

"Are you feeling itchy?" I ask.

"What kind of monster would pair up cheese and broccoli in water? Yuck," they reply.

If I thought it was silly, the quiz idea, now I see its value. People do activities on dates, they go for a walk, or to the cinema and a restaurant. When you're online dating you do none of that, the only thing left is to talk about ourselves which can give a false sense of intimacy. The quiz takes it all, it's an activity we are doing together, as silly as it is.

"French onion soup?" the red letters read. "I swear I'm not a fussy eater but…"

"Yeah," I agree. "Even I have to give that one a Yuck."

We talk a little more about soups, they always have a comment and it always makes me laugh. This little spark comes alive right when I can't stop laughing from their comment about chilled cucumber soup. I had never got to this point right here, when the conversation is easy, when I get excited for more. It sounds strange because I had boyfriends before, but the spark only lasted the first date. It was like after that I just kept dating because they hadn't given me a reason to stop.

I wonder if I did the whole dating thing wrong, if what I should have done was to look for a reason to continue dating.

"I'm the jokester," I tell them when we finish the quiz.

"Are you though?"

"No," and I laugh. "I mean, I have a good sense of humour I guess, but I hate to be the centre of attention."

"I never thought about that, if I wanted to be the centre of attention or not."

"Isn't that odd? Shouldn't it be something you have figure out about yourself?"

I see red is taking a second to reply. I wonder if I struck a nerve. I know we aren't allowed to have deep meaningful conversations, but sometimes it heads this way regardless.

"I think I'm too busy for self-contemplation," the answer finally comes.

I am about to type, but more comes through, "This is not saying I don't think it's important, or that I think I'm better than the rest because I'm self- absorbed and too busy. Am I coming off ok still?"

I give a little smile to the screen, once more my attention to the crew around me just comes back when Michael gently comes forward with the camera.

"I actually thought it was a little sad to be too busy for self-contemplation."

I see three red dots blinking once and twice, I regret what I wrote, maybe we are standing in a point when it's too easy to misunderstand each other.

"I wish I could have a proper conversation with you," they say.

I breathe slowly in relief.

"How come? Pleasantries and BuzzFeed quizzes aren't cutting anymore?"

"We can come back to them any time. You sound like a good person, who I would appreciate to have a normal conversation with."

And I just type back, "Soon."

Producer: *Can you please state to the camera the three things you told Dr Bernard were the most important to you?*

The other camera man is named Steve, the makeup artist on set is Moira and the intern is Cathal. I know them now, since the problem with the other producer, and I'm glad I do. I can tell they are a team that works well together. Moira told me, while she painted my face, that they all worked for the network so they worked together in a show or the other. As I suspected, they have a great respect for Kelly, more so than for the director whose name is Ed.

"They are salivating over you and your match, you know?" Moira whispered to me while going over my lashes with mascara. "Kelly said you are going to be the fan favourite. She's betting on it."

I'm not sure I want to be a fan favourite, the thought of fans and people actually watching while I'm on a date makes my stomach drop. I think about my mother, who called me yesterday to ask how things were and if I would be open to be set on a date with her boring friend, Susan's, son, Eric. I said no. She wanted to know why and I had nothing to say but I had met Eric when we were kids and he's as much of a boring snob as his mother.

Mother wasn't happy about that. She claimed people like Eric and Susan were our people, the ones I grew up with and understand my life. I know what she thinks about me volunteering at the hospital and my friends from there. She was happy when I was going twice a week for a couple of hours but when started to look like a job... let's say she wasn't comfortable with that.

A permanent position was offered to me plenty of times. My friend Maria says I would be the head nurse at this rate if I had just taken a job.

I love the hospital. I love my friends and being a full-time nurse would be a dream coming true. And why I don't go for it?

I'm back to the present and the intense lights are back on me, the computer is right in front of me and I had almost forgotten to be excited to chat with those little red letters.

I don't think much about who my perfect match is. When I read Dr Bernard's research, I thought that would get me anxious at some point. At the same time, I wanted to be part of the program. I was expecting to be confronted by many feelings regarding of my match.

It never happened, though. I never had a moment to wonder that I came from a family who only cared about appearances and I'm on a dating show where that's the least important of all.

Once the crew is ready, Kelly asks me about the list I gave to Dr Bernard.

"Kindness. I said I wanted to me with someone who cares about other people. Compatibility, sense of humour and silly things like that can make life so much better. And political views, of course."

Kelly nods and she signals to the laptop in front of me, I look as the red talks first once more.

"They tell me today is the day, are you ready?"

"What's the chances we disagree on everything that matters?" I ask.

"Then the show is officially a prank," the letters read.

I smile at the screen. I feel Michael's camera right on me, but it isn't news at this point. Little by little I got accustomed to the lights, to Kelly's instructions and the makeup. I'm not able to completely switch off, but I'm calmer now, and might be because the red letters always get me smiling silly.

"What are the three most important things to you?" I ask.

The answer takes a second to come through, it is a loaded question and I didn't expect anything but.

"Social responsibility, political views and science over religion," red tells me.

Very close to mine and so clinical that makes me wonder if

red isn't a scientist of some sort. I know I'm not supposed to make assumptions, I rather like the idea of freeing myself of any physical and status like expectations, but with such a clear answer is hard not to go there.

"What about you?" they ask.

"Kindness, sense of humour and political views," I laugh a little with myself as I type, "I think I prefer yours."

Red replies right away, "Kindness. I made it boring with the social responsibility bit but that's what I was thinking when I put it down. I wanted to be around someone that sometimes cries with the news, is that a weird thing to say?"

It is, I think to myself and I nod to no one. However, I can completely relate.

"I get you," I simply type.

"I have the same feeling you do."

I'd manage throughout this process barely talking when the cameras are rolling. I know they have just a few minutes of recording of my interactions and every second counts.

"What else can we talk about?" I ask Kelly, turning to see her. She is following our conversation of course and looks up when I address her.

"Anything," she says. "Don't give away too much of your appearance, gender or social status. That's all."

"But I can ask about family and all?"

"Yes."

It's all I've ever wanted. Ask about a billion things that I couldn't do the last two times.

But before I think where to start, they send me a message. "Have you notice when we weren't allowed to talk about anything, anything was all we could think of. Now I wish we had a BuzzFeed quiz."

"The process makes sense when you think about how close we are even after just chatting twice," I send and then something comes over me and I shake my head, "I'm sorry, I mean I feel close to you at least."

"Yes, I agree," they reply at the same time I send my last message.

Deciding to go ahead, I ask, "Do you have any siblings?"

"Two older brothers," they tell me. "And you?"

"One younger brother."

Their reply comes quick this time as well, "I won't get too much into it but my brothers are stupid."

I giggled and type, "Aren't you scared they watch the show?"

"I hope they do," red says and I laugh again, "Is your brother stupid?"

I think about how to describe Dennis, I wouldn't say he's stupid, the word itself would crush him and my mom whose full time job is to fuss over him. Instead, I say, "He's the family baby, he can't do no wrong."

I think it's vague enough not to get me into trouble with

mom and Dennis, but enough to make them understand.

"How diplomatic of you," the reply comes.

I chuckle because I know I've been caught, they are right, vague and diplomatic is very McKenna of me.

"Does your family support you to be on this show?" I ask.

"No," they say straight away.

I rub my hands into each other, we have that in common as well. I see three red dots coming and going, as they aren't sure what to tell me.

Eventually, "I'm old enough to be ok if they don't support all my decisions. I'd made peace with it many years ago."

I want to ask for more, but it comes to me that maybe they are being vague for a reason, the delay on a reply was probably their way to type that without giving too much away.

Instead of questioning more, I just say, "My family doesn't know I applied. I'm sure they won't be happy and I definitely did not made peace with upsetting them. But that's future me problem, uh?"

"I can walk you through it," they offer. "I will teach you how to be a disappointment."

It's that dry sarcastic humour that makes me laugh out loud again. I find easy to find kinship in someone I know nothing about it and I had never seen.

"Do you want to talk about if we are going to the next part?"

they ask, and I'm almost too distracted to understand for a second.

But it comes to me eventually, yes, we have to decide if we want to go to the second part of the experiment, if we want to meet in person.

I get butterflies straight away, it's like asking someone you like on a date when you have no idea what they feel about you. I'm not an idiot, I know we are laughing and the banter is great, but that doesn't mean they see me in a sexual way.

Which is odd, I think to myself. I've never met this person. I don't know anything about them and still I know right in my bones what I have been doing is pure flirting. I'm not trying to be a friend; I'm not just being funny and nice as I would to anyone.

I bite my lip and my hands hover over the keyboard. I want to say something clever that would make them want to go out with me, but my mind is blank.

"If means anything to you," the message comes through while my hands still not doing anything typing, "I think you're fantastic. I'm left chuckling after you log off, just the thought of seeing you in person and being able to actually date you?"

They leave it like that and I start a frenetic typing, I know they are typing as well.

"I really want to go out with you!" I say at the same time they say, "Can we go out, please?"

My smile is gigantic and when I look around, the whole crew

is smiling right back at me.

Producer: *You know what to do, Gigi.*

I sit on the usual white chair. Cathal fixed me with the mic and Moira already fussed over me with a brush.

"Just send him over to the hospital," I tell Michael. "He can see for himself how the day to day is, you know?"

Michael's son wants to pursue medicine, he will graduate from secondary school in two years, but Michael thinks he's only watching too much TV and doesn't understand how much work and sacrifice comes with a career as a doctor.

"Would you scare him, Gigi?" he asks and I laugh.

"I can show him around, introduce him to the nurses and the doctors and he can see on his own. It's not very glamourous and has much more poop involved than you would like."

Michael chuckles and says he will take me on it. It's funny to think how we got here, how one day they were intimidating TV people, and now they call me Gigi and ask about my life.

Kelly told me last night, after me and my perfect match decided on seeing each other face to face, that they have a crew party to celebrate going to the next phase.

We, the cast, will have a week off and the crew will get everything organised to the next step. I'm invited to go out with them. First I was afraid it would be something I shouldn't be part of, but Kelly says it will be in her house and no one big from the network will be attending.

I would love to analyse the situation, but I'm sure I have to be a licensed therapist to do so. I want to be friends with them, they are lovely people and I'm happy to have met them. Still, it's one more group of people who I'm part of and not really part of.

At the hospital, I'm not a medical professional. I have lot of pull because the staff knows me for years and they trust me and I trust them, plus my dad donated money to Oldmill Memorial plenty of times and the board eats from his hand.

That's the same way I'm not part of the TV show's crew, and I wonder how many participants had flourished a friendship with the crew, how many people call the producer by name like I do.

I shake my head and look ahead, to the little red light from Michael's camera, to Kelly's signal for me to start.

They want me to give a little summary of what were my first impressions of my match, so I start, "I thought it was going to be weird, being on a date to have people watching you and following your conversation but it was actually pretty ok." I laugh and I see their smiles as well. "Dating someone without knowing their physical attributes and gender…I honestly think it's the easiest part. It felt natural because I would normally be concerned about the other stuff anyway, but I felt free to ask." I bite the side of my mouth, I know it isn't very attractive, but I do it out of habit.

"Each time I am on a date, it comes to this moment when I want to ask all the important stuff but I know it is socially unacceptable to do so. I want to ask the real questions, never mind a checklist of what they want for the future, sometimes I just want to ask…" I shake my head. "Are you upset by the news like I am? Do you feel empathy when see people working under unfair conditions? Do you inform yourself and listen to the opinions of people from different communities than yours or do you just make opinions based on your own set of beliefs and lack of experience?"

I stop for a second and look straight at the camera. "That's usually frowned upon. We are expected to be pleasant and be a good dinner company. It felt good to have that expectation taken out of me. I guess it feels good to be as unpleasant as I can."

The favourite couple of WNB's Dating Blind!

The couple who had you swoon every Sunday is finally ready to meet in person. While a couple of fan favourites didn't make into the second phase of the show, the whole nation rejoiced when Gianna smiled right into the camera after being asked on a date.

Of all Dating Blind's contestants Gianna always played with the public's heartstrings with her sweet smile and unwavering belief in goodness. There's no viewer who didn't cheer for her every online encounter and hoped it would be a happy ending to the small-town hospital volunteer.

This Sunday Gianna will finally meet her perfect match and the nation holds its breath in anticipation.

Tune in at 9pm on WNB for a brand-new episode of Dating Blind.

Producer: *This way, Nadia.*

She looks kinder than the one I usually have. I can tell by the delicate smile, as she genuinely cares if my mate and I get our happy ending.

I look down at my outfit and breathe in and out. They told me not to over dress and yet I overthought every step of the way. My best mate Ramira, who is the only person who knows about *Dating Blind*, made me promise to wear my mint green and gold kameez when meeting my match for the first time. I hope she's right.

"You look great," says the kind producer and I smile a little at her.

I find it funny, the necessity of people talking about our appearances. I was baffled to discover I was going to be wearing makeup and have a hairdresser to carefully pull my hair out every single day to be on a show that its premise is how physical image isn't important.

I know Dr Bernard is genuine. I followed her research for a couple of years and got in contact with her when I left London to take over the hospital. She knows I believe in her papers and that's why I was asked to be on the show. Granted Dr Bernard is an intelligent and very capable woman, I know very little about the showrunners of *Dating Blind*. After weeks dealing with the most repugnant human being of a producer, I'm comfortable to say many aspects of Dr Bernard's research will be compromised to fit WNB's agenda.

I followed through because of them. Because of the person behind the screen, with the perfect sense of humour, that person who made me almost fall in love after only a couple of online conversations.

After my first meeting, Shay—Dr Bernard—called to ask me what I thought about my match. I wondered if it was against the show's policy, or even contradictory to her own results, but at the same time I felt like a girl replaying a first date with a friend over the phone.

I've never been so certain she's right. Attraction and love are deeper than the sense of physicality, of what the eyes can see. People have been falling in love online for years, and the reason is that words are the most powerful thing in the world.

I breathe deeply letting the air come slowly out of my lungs and I nod at the producer in front of me. Her hand is on the door handle in front of us and I know they are there already, waiting for me.

As the door slowly opens, I see the usual *Dating Blind* set, the blinding white and gold that I'm almost certain is the reason why the show gets its name.

The crew is positioned in place, the lights over one single person sitting in a white chair, with the other chair just beside.

I take a step back and gasp. My hands open and close and I frown in confusion. I try to settle the creases in my forehead, I don't want anyone to think I'm anything but surprised.

Her curly redded frame turns to me and the vibrant blue eyes are wide in surprise. She's wearing a pretty dark turquoise dress that buttons down to her small feet wearing white trainers.

My mouth goes dry, but I try to speak either way, the words come out gravel on my throat, I know I sound weird and she might notice but I need the verbal confirmation otherwise I might go insane.

"Gianna?" I say.

She steps forward, I see a camera follow her movement and then she says in her usual sweet voice, "Dr Singh?"

Producer: *Do you know each other?*

A silence follows after the producer's question. I look at Gianna and let her take the lead. I watch as her mouth opens and closes, with closed eyes she sighs, "We... Dr Singh is the head physician at the hospital where I volunteer," she tells the producer.

"Nadia," I clear my throat, "My name is Nadia."

Gianna bobs her head, like she's convincing herself to call me such. For the first time I'm insecure about the process. All the possibilities never bothered me, man, woman, non-binary, able-bodied or not. I wanted to find love and I wanted to love find me, the package wasn't important and I knew it wasn't.

However, I never thought about how to go around a situation like this one we see ourselves in. When someone who looks at me everyday like some kind of a boss is the same person who laughed with me about my hatred of soup.

Gianna closes her eyes and takes another breath, she says, looking directly at the producer between us, "Can we have five minutes to talk, Kelly? Without the cameras?"

I thought she was going to get a flat no. Obviously, you don't get to make a reality show if you are ok in giving such allowances. But before the words were even out of her mouth both camera men already had their equipment lowered.

I watch in awe as the producer agrees, and all the crew seems to be so understanding, "Five minutes, Gigi," pleads Kelly.

Gigi.

That's what they call her around the hospital too. They always have a smile on their faces when they say it, even the senior staff asks her for help from time to time.

I remember when I was transferred, to Oldmill Memorial. I knew it was a huge step up for me; I was young and I was already the chief physician even if I had to give up London and move to a small town in Ireland called Oldmill. The name itself sounded stupid, there were no Mills to be found.

I was instructed by the board. I worked long enough at hospitals to know I was supposed to ignore the board, but, in the end, they had great information. I was to replace Dr Abram, an asshole who used to refuse to perform abortions and discriminated patients and staff alike. The board wasn't happy to remove him, they didn't possess much conscience.

It was a lawyer from a village even smaller than Oldmill who start gathering testimonials from the staff of Dr Abram's dirty deeds. And while usually that never goes anywhere, a little

Miss Thing who volunteered at the hospital for years, came forward and was going to be called as main witness.

"I can't start explaining how this is bad for all of us..." said a severe-looking woman who I wasn't in the mood into learning the name.

"Sure look," explained the other dinosaur of the board. "There's always complains, uh? But you don't need John McKenna's daughter starting a lawsuit against you."

I agreed because I wasn't interested in knowing the views of the board. That night I googled John McKenna and read everything it was possible about him.

The fortune, the farms, the six digits donations to the hospital. A daughter named Gianna and a son named Dennis.

I liked the idea that someone stood up against Dr Abram, and the fact the pressure came from someone with a powerful father was probably the reason why they needed to take Dr Abram down and bring me, a much younger woman of colour. That piece of the puzzle made sense now.

However, the character of Gianna remained confusing. As admirable her instance against him was, I wasn't a fan of people who came from money. Specially the type of money the McKennas had.

When I met Gianna, I had no idea what to expect. Everything I knew about her was contradictory, but I had never expected someone like her. Soft spoken, capable. Clearly adored among the whole staff.

    In the full year since I took the position of Oldmill's head physician, I've been wondering why is she not permanent staff? Why isn't she a nurse or a doctor? Why was Gianna McKenna so difficult to figure out?

"We don't have much time…"

Gianna grabs my hand and drags me out of the room, she looks both sides making us stop and I remind her we don't have much time. Out of the choices and with the clock running out, she brings me into a small closet, closes the door and turns on the light.

"What you think we should do?" she asks me quickly.

I shrug, "I don't know."

"It never crossed my mind I would meet someone here I knew."

"Same," I nod and cross my arms. "But again, I don't know many people."

She's on a roll. "Even if we back out, they have footage of us talking, they can air that anyway. The whole hospital will know…"

"You never thought about the possibility that our colleagues would watch it?"

She looks up at me, we are almost the same height usually but she's wearing trainers and I'm in my green high heels. She's frowning and I see when she bites her lower lip.

I shift uncomfortably. Shay Bernard would love this right here: I've known Gianna for a full year, and of course I've noticed she's a good-looking woman, but it's only after having the time to talk to her in this experiment that apparently I start to follow the movement of her teeth grazing her lip.

Her big blue eyes widen a little more if was that possible. "I don't mind anyone to see me in this show. I mean, I wouldn't have applied if I did. But... you're my boss."

"No, I'm not."

"This isn't Grey's Anatomy, you know?" she continues.

"I'm well aware," I nod.

"I don't want you to lose your authority!" she gasps, "And everyone will think they..."

"They can also date me?"

She whips her head to me and breathes out. I step forward and place my hands on her shoulders. She shakes a bit under my fingers, but I'm resolute into trying to show her reason.

"We've never been this close," Gianna whispers.

"You've never locked me in a closet before," I joke, but it doesn't land so I continue, "You're asking yourself the wrong questions. What you should be asking is if you want to see me again."

Her eyes find mine and her bottom lip bobbles. I'm really putting myself out there but I reckon one of us needs to ask the hard question. We got into this programme to find someone to share a life with, independently of anything else. We all agreed that the most important part of romance wasn't what was on the outside. Gianna had to decide if she still believed in that.

I hold my breath, but eventually she nods. And then with a small voice she asks, "Do you want to see me again?"

I chuckle a little, "Yes, Gianna, I want to. I think we can get along as soon as you stop freaking out."

That makes her laugh and I'm pleased. I've been imagining how her laugh sounds like since I'd started exchanging messages with those purple letters.

Who would have thought, the laugh I wanted to hear so much, was the same one I heard every day?

Producer: *Can we try again?*

To my absolute horror, they make us do the reveal again. I'm against it, but Gianna says she prefers to try once more than having the old one aired.

She's right. We try once more, and even though my delivery is rather robotic, Gianna looks happy to see me this time around.

"You're still going to have to touch the subject you both know each other," Kelly says to us after the reveal bit was done. "People will figure it out once it's aired. They will probably know from the start, when your names come along."

I look to my side and I can see Gianna is getting nervous all over again. "That sounds bad, Kelly."

The producer laughs and waves her hand. "No, no, I think it's great actually! They will be watching day after day to see the exact moment you both figure it out."

Something comes to me. As Kelly said, people will know from the beginning. People in the experiment know too, after all they have our files, they know my place of work and they probably know everything there is to know about Gianna.

Whoever paired us up together also knew.

The rest of the interview goes in a blur, we answer questions and tell them we are excited for the first date. Kelly tries to dig more than necessary about the whole working together issue, but Gianna is surprisingly firm with her answers and doesn't let any room for speculation.

When our interview ends, we are taken apart. They tell us it's important that they document all our interactions from now on, but that just sounds too much on the controlling side of things.

Gianna is taken through one door and I'm take through the other. She looks back and mouths me "bye," waving her finger slowly at me.

I expect Shay will decline my request to see her, but she doesn't. I thought she would lecture me about the integrity of the experiment, but she doesn't. On the contraire, Shay asks me to meet her in my hotel lobby for a drink. I'm there at six on the dot.

"Always punctual," she says sitting in front of me, "Some would call it OCD."

I frown. "That's an odd diagnose. What are you having?"

She looks at my wine glass, I'm having chardonnay, and she asks for the same from the waitress.

"Did you know?" as soon as the order bit is finished.

"No," she doesn't miss a beat.

"Shay…"

"Of course I learned it eventually, but I wasn't aware at the beginning. I told the team you were a friend and I didn't want to match you myself."

"When did you learn?"

Shay rolls her head and taps her fingers on the wooden table, "As soon as you were matched, of course."

"So Gianna was to be my match regardless?"

"Of course!" she sounds offended.

"I had to check, Shay! The producers are salivating over the story, I know they're going to milk it for what is worth…"

"Are you uncomfortable about that?" Her wine arrives and she takes a sip.

I wave her question away. "Of course not. I knew I was getting into a reality show. Have you read their contracts?"

Shay low whistles and I chuckle. "As long as it wasn't fabricated for ratings…"

She makes a noise from deep of her throat. "I wouldn't put my reputation on the line for ratings, would I? And I wouldn't mess with a friend for it either."

I sip the wine and let it go slowly down my throat.

"Besides that, are you happy?" she asks me.

I can't stop myself and I crack my neck, Shay laughs, she always says is my tension tic.

"I'm not in love with the fact she's a McKenna. It's messy enough without her daddy being the biggest benefactor of the hospital."

"Are they bigots?" Shay asks point blanc.

I shrug. "I assume the worst of wealthy families, if they are, the board won't be very happy, will they? I can lose my job."

Shay thinks about that for a second and nods her head. "That's true. You should talk to her, away from the cameras."

I watch her, she knows we aren't allowed to contact the other participants, even though I know they are all scattered around the very same hotel they put me in. I had played that game before, watching the people coming and going from the lobby and tried to guess who would be just a tourist and who's a single ready to mingle.

"I can get you her extension number," Shay says calmly.

"You know that would be a violation of the contract…"

"Fuck the network, Nadia," she says surprisingly. "If this is going to make you lose your job then you've got to figure it out now."

I think about what she says. I know she's correct, but I can't think of what I could do to help it.

DATING BLIND

"They will still air the bits they have already, Shay," I say trying my best to not show resentment in my voice.

"Shit..." she says shaking her head, "Well, we'll deal if we have to. God knows I know some bastards in high places since this all started. I'll pull some strings."

I laugh and drink the rest of my drink, "Get me the room number then."

"This is not allowed"

She whispers, and it's adorable. I bite my whole mouth trying to avoid any sigh to come out.

After Shay got me her room number, I played with what to say to her for long. I didn't want to come out and ask if her parents were bigots, I didn't even want to address the fact to everyone this would be a gay relationship and I was afraid to hear what were her thoughts about that.

"We just need to talk for a second ok?" I say to her.

She hesitates, "I know. We can't go over this whole situation with cameras on our faces, can we?"

This was my chance, but I let it pass. "Are you feeling better about the whole thing?"

She giggles on the other side. "I always loved your accent, it's funny to hear it right in my hear."

Funny wouldn't be the word I would use, but I try to let it go.

"They say I have a posh accent," I tell her.

"I know. Did anyone say that to you?"

"Maria," I confess, "She was helping me during a procedure and she told me to stop talking posh to her."

Gianna laughs, I know she and Maria are close, "She can't handle it…" and she breathes, "It's going to be weird calling you Nadia."

"Of everything going on, that's the part you're finding difficult?"

I can imagine Gianna in her hotel room. I hear the bed when she sits down to talk to me, I smile thinking about the way she gets flustered.

"Ahh…" she exhales. "I'm trying a few things to not to get overwhelmed."

I don't want to overwhelm her, of course I don't. Even if we weren't in this together, before the show and before I was attracted to her. Gianna is a good person, it was easy to see she never wished ill of anyone. It's clear as day that everyone who get to know her, loves her. So even before all this, I would never wish to put her in an uncomfortable position.

"What's overwhelming you?"

"It's silly but I never thought it through the whole being on the telly thing, you know? I read Dr Bernard's research and I was sure she's right, I wanted to be part of it. I just never really put that much thought in the reality show bit."

"Did you have a tough time with the solo interviews?"

"A little," she says, "I didn't want to sound stupid."

"I bet you didn't."

"You're being nice."

"No, I *know* you."

I hear her deep breath and she replies, "I know," at the same time I say, "I'm sorry."

"You have nothing to be sorry for," Gianna tells me.

"I'm trying to not overwhelm you more than…"

"Nadia," she breathes my name. "I knew what I signed up for. The telly part was hard and I got used to it. Seeing you made me think of all the people who we both know that will be watching us… My parents, my brother…"

There was no better opportunity than that. She mentioned her parents, there it's the best opportunity I can wish for.

"Gianna… How you think your parents will react to all of this? Do they know?"

Silence in the other end, my heart waits.

"They don't know," she tells me.

"If you were to guess…"

"My mother is difficult and my dad…" she trails off and it's almost what I need to lose hope. I steady my voice and explain.

"You know your dad knows a few members of the board

and…"

Gianna gasps, I know she's connecting the dots and I don't like how terrified she might be.

"What do you think the reaction will be?"

"I… I… I don't know…" she says and I can tell she's lost, "Do you think the board…?"

"They aren't exactly loyal people."

I want to say the board will value her dad's money much more than my work, but I bite my tongue and don't say it. There's no reason why to say such a thing, it doesn't matter how true it is.

"And you're worried they will fire you if my dad asks?"

I want to say yes, but in the end my silence is enough for her.

"I won't let it happen, Nadia," she sighs pure courage. "It just won't happen. We all hated how things went when Dr Abram was around. Since you started working, things changed so much, for the better. It's just not the fact it's not fair and I want to be with you and…."

"Do you want to be with me?"

"I… I…" she stops herself a little, I chuckle on the other end. "What I mean is the hospital deserves a head physician like you. The nurses adore you. The patients tell me how a great diagnostician you are. Oldmill Memorial won't be losing you."

I'm out of words. I know the staff likes me alright but I never heard Gianna talk so passionately, especially about me. My head goes for a complete spin and I feel my heart beating rapidly in my chest.

"Thank you," I croak.

"It's ok, it's just the truth."

"Thank you. Either way, it's sweet," I clear my throat and roll my eyes to myself. I have to get better at this.

I know I have to let her go, but I don't want to, she's not saying anything and I feel in my bones is time to say goodbye.

"What room are you in?" She asks.

"Thirty-three," I tell her.

"That's so close."

"I know."

More silence.

"We can…" she pauses, "Escape for a second. Julius minds our floor and he has a break at half-twelve."

"How on earth do you know the name of the man who surveys our floor?"

"I talk to people…" She answers simply.

I chuckle, "Alright then…"

"Alright?"

"Yep. Half-twelve?"

"Half-twelve."

"Knock knock"

She doesn't knock, the smile comes out easily to my lips when Gianna whispers the word, and soon I hear the steps moving away.

I wait for half a second before I try the door, and even though I know she just passed my door, I open it fearfully, watching left to right. And to my right, down the corridor, I see the bushy ginger hair peeking out the corner. I rush my steps to meet her and the strong feeling of mischief takes over me.

I was never rebellious, of course. I grew with two strong-willed brothers who, unfortunately, were never bright enough to entice me into any wrong doings. I knew we would be discovered eventually, and I wasn't dumb enough to entertain them.

Throughout the years I watched Aryan and Dev getting themselves into trouble and I have to admit that's a big part of why I became such a stickler for rules. And if I thought for a second it was because I disliked it, while I tip toed to meet Gianna, I knew that was a lie I had told myself.

I simply never had someone to share it with.

Gianna takes my hand and we run; I hold myself not to giggle. I try my best to remember I am in my thirties.

She takes me rushing down the stairs and then to the back door; we slip out without anyone seeing us and I'm starting to wonder why I ever thought this was secure to start with.

"Do you think we are messing up the research?" she whispers to me.

"Solitude is a network thing because they want us to have all interactions in front of the camera. That's nothing to do with the actual experiment."

"Hmm," she says. I notice we still holding hands, but I don't say anything.

I let her guide me until we reach the back garden, a few steps leading the outside entertainment, a pool inside a glass house.

"They are so concerned we won't swim after hours…" she says pointing at the big chains looped into the glass house's door, and a massive lock. "They forget to properly lock the rest of it. Come here…"

We pass the glass house and I look to the beautiful blue pool inside. Even locked inside doors, it glistens under the moon. Maybe they have a point, whoever they might be. The pool is enticing enough to attract all guests after hours.

Once we circle it to the back, Gianna takes me a couple of

steps up a small leading to the parking lot. That's where she sits, pointing to the two lighting polls closest to us. "No cameras, see?"

I sit too. "When is our floor's security coming back?"

"He has only a ten-minute break every two hours. So, we have to slip in then."

She never told me that part though, the part we had to be out for two hours. I try not to worry, it's a warm enough night, clear sky and a warm breeze, those are so rare I should feel privileged.

"How do you know all of this?" I ask.

"Jeff smokes," she explains like I know who Jeff is, "He's trying to stop though…"

Gianna leans back and tip her head up to the sky. She sighs like it's the most relaxed she had ever been and I can't stop the little curving of my own lips. "Tell me, why did you decide to be part of the show?" I ask.

She looks at me, but just for a second, and she's back watching the stars. "I read Dr Bernard's full research and interviews… I think she's brilliant. A true feminist."

I chuckle. "You sound like a groupie."

"It is time scientists have groupies," she jokes.

"When this whole thing is over, I can bring you for a couple of drinks with Shay and you can fan over her."

Gianna turns her head to me and I open a smile, I slip that in so calmly and it has its desired effect.

"Why do you call Dr Bernard by her first name?"

"We are friends."

Gianna groans and I chuckle. "Are you serious?"

"It started the same way as you. I read a few articles by her in a medical paper and got in contact because I thought they were interesting. We sent a few emails back and forth and yes… I ended up having dinner at her house a couple of times."

Gianna looks at me deeply and shakes her head, "Don't make me hate you, Nadia."

I laugh, but my heart skips a beat. The easy way she calls me by my name gives me a little hope that maybe we can go around this whole Doctor-Volunteer issue of ours.

"You shouldn't hate me. I told you I can introduce you two. But I have to warn you, she is happily married."

She laughs and I smile, am I trying too much? I can't tell. Since Gianna was revealed to be the purple letters who wrote to me, it's like all made sense. I saw her every day for a whole year, I try to stay away, knowing who her father is, knowing what happened to the last head physician who crossed her, and still every night after work I caught myself with a glass of wine wondering what was up with Gianna McKenna.

If it wasn't for *Dating Blind*, I would never act on anything, and I know she wouldn't too. She always treated me with respect and kept me at a cold distance that at first I thought I understood. Later, as I watched her warm manner towards everyone in her life, it made me wonder why was I singled out.

Those two people were the same, the easy talk, witty humour, called my perfect match and the beautiful volunteer of the hospital I worked. Those two pieces were Gianna and I kept biting my tongue not to ask everything about her.

"Why did you apply for the show?" She asks.

I shrug. "I didn't. Shay invited me, she knew I believed in everything she had written and mostly I believed the reality show idea was a quick way to put the word out there. To make it mainstream."

Gianna nods. "I thought about that. Why would Dr Bernard let WNB turn her research into…this."

I sit back, my back to the hard concrete of the steps, my arms resting on my bending knees. "She wasn't a fan of the idea initially. The first time WNB approached her they got a flat no, of course. Specially because they weren't thinking in doing a documentary, no, it was the lowest form of television." I chuckle. "But Orlando changed her mind."

"Who's Orlando?"

"The other Dr Bernard," I tell her. "Shay's husband. He made a point that a reality show would bring her idea to the head of millions, right now was only being read by intellectuals and doctors, but when you display like that on TV… The publicity, the interview opportunities. How many people wouldn't change the way they date just from watching the show?"

I watch Gianna biting her lip and nodding. "That's very romantic don't you think? All of this is to make people be open for love?"

I shrug. "It will change the life of many people, yes, if they can just fall in love with what is important. But also, it was an opportunity to change the face of TV a little…"

"What do you mean?"

"When Shay accepted the offer, she asked to be responsible for the matching of course, and to work with her own team. She also wanted the casting to be open to everyone."

"Everyone?" Gianna asks a little confused.

"Everyone. She was adamant about it. The most important part of *Dating Blind* was to accept everyone who was open enough. It wasn't about looking good on TV or having enough Instagram followers."

"I'm surprised WNB accepted."

"Me too," I confess and she smiles at me.

"And she invited you to be in? Just like that?"

"Yes, and wasn't sure about the reality TV part, but I was the first one to agree with Orlando when he said she had to accept WNB's offer, so she asked me to put money where my mouth is."

Gianna smiles. "Do you regret it?"

"No."

Producer: *Just act natural, try to forget we are here.*

I can see by Gianna's face she must be thinking the same thing that I am: forgetting the cameras are here will be impossible. The place is packed with them, people dressed in black with polo shirts with *Dating Blind*'s logo everywhere. Bringing coffee, retouching make up, setting up microphones, getting lights ready.

If I thought our head interviews were uncomfortable, that was absolutely nothing in comparison to this circus.

I look at Gianna and she looks terrified. I wish I could calm her down, but I'm feeling the same pressure.

We're in the official *Dating Blind* restaurant, with all the other couples who decided to remain and date for a little longer in front of the cameras. This is supposed to be our first date after we reveal ourselves to each other, all the producers keep reminding us the mood today is romance, but they fail to realise there's nothing romantic about being told what's the mood should be.

Gianna squeezes my hand and I turn to look at her, "Have you heard?" she whispers, I shake my head, "They say a girl on the other floor left because her match was too ugly. How awful is that?"

At this point we had figured out we were placed in little pools of people for organisation purposes. Our floor has three matches, us, Jeff and Natalie and Trevor and Josh. Happily all three couples are still here, but our floor is one of the few. Most floors have just one couple, I know above us has only one because I saw them coming down the lift the other day.

Now that we have seen each other's faces, WNB doesn't seem to care we know who is on the show or not. We still can't talk or hang out at the hotel, but everyone on our floor gets in a van together for filming, and that's a huge improvement.

I shake my head. "How do people know that?"

"She told everyone, during the reveal. Her match is devastated, they were promised to return next season."

I frown at the mention of a next season. I didn't know Shay was considering, we had talked about it and she told me WNB would not even talk about it until they knew how the first season went. But nothing was aired yet, so how would they be able to promise a second season to anyone?

We are guided to the side of the restaurant and have one of the crew explain what the intent of the early start is. We will be walking for the morning.

A few people groan, Gianna included, but I can't be much surprised. It's way too early to expect us to sit down and have dinner. However, I understand the frustration. We aren't actors. We want to find love and what is the probability of having a romantic dinner when you are shooting since six in the morning?

We are led to a warehouse across the street, they are filming per couple and there's no point in having us around in the background. In the long table right in the middle of the warehouse we find cold pastries, and weak coffee. I get a cup of tea for me and Gianna, she's talking to Jeff and Natalie and they are laughing like old friends.

I bring the styrofoam cup to her and she smiles in gratitude. I insert myself in the group, Jeff is telling them something and Natalie and Gianna have big smiles on their faces.

It is a tale about his work colleagues and I don't understand the resolution but I stand there anyway. When the silence comes for a second and my anxiety kicks in, Josh and Trevor join our group.

"Do you know how many people started with us?" Josh asks.

They all shrug, but I say, "Thirty-two."

Gianna turns to me, she knows I'm friends with Shay and I would have more information than the regular participant, but I'm glad she reveals nothing to the others.

Josh looks around the place, counting people. I look around with him, it's alarming when you start to count just the people without black polo shirts.

"We all heard that story with the girl who decided not to go through it when she saw her bloke…" Trevor is saying.

"Thirty-two people are sixteen couples, right?" Natalie starts.

"Assuming that they are subscribing into the societal pressure of monogamic coupling…" says Josh.

I hold a laugh, Natalie frowns at him, "Yeah, let's go with that…"

"I bet some people gave up while they were still chatting online," Gianna says, "If they didn't click right away…"

"I thought this was a sure thing," Jeff scratches his cheek.

"Nothing is certain when you're dealing with humans," I weigh in. "Of course I believe S…Dr Bernard's matching is flawless, but even I know if I wasn't really invested in meeting someone, not even Gianna would be enough to make me stay."

She beams at me, like that was the best complement someone had ever given her. "Plus we have to consider many people are paired up with the same sex and maybe they aren't ready for that."

She shuffles in place and I get nervous again. It's the bucket of cold water I never needed. Gianna looks certain about the program, she even looks certain about me, but I can't let myself forget about her parents and what it can do to my career.

I should've asked her about it last night while we talked for hours outside. It was the perfect moment to question her if she had ever dated a woman, if she was ready to do it so publicly. However, more and more I get seduced by the illusion of having no problems, nothing on our way. The idea of staying out there under the moon talking seemed much better than having a conversation that could be the end of everything.

I try to get out of my own head and participate with the conversation, but every time I look at Gianna I wonder if the person she says isn't ready, is herself.

When it's our turn to be filmed arriving at the restaurant, I do it on autopilot. It's probably for the best, otherwise I know I would feel too awkward.

When they announce is lunch time, Gianna turns to me with a wavery smile, "Are you ok?" and I surprise myself telling her, "No."

Director: *Is everyone ready?*

Between walking towards the door, eventually filming us arriving and asking for a table, and then meeting us, by the time we are sitting at our table is dinner time.

We all look amazing; the makeup crew did wonders for a bunch of cranky people absolutely tired of stale pastries and gross coffee. None of us looks as tired as we feel.

With the comings and goings of the day, I didn't have the time to explain myself to Gianna, so I simply sounded awfully high maintenance being upset and refusing to talk about it.

The next couple of hours is supposed to be natural; the reality in the reality TV. The waiters come around and take our orders, the cameras dance between the tables and record snaps of our conversations.

"What's going on?" Gianna asks when the camera moves on after filming the servers taking our order.

"I'm worried," I confess.

"What are you worried about?" She frowns, but a crew member passes and she says, "Do you drink red or white?"

I watch as the crew member goes. "They still have the sound," I say, which is true, there's no secrets when they have microphones stuck on our backs.

"And they are going to just air my whispers and no image? This is not illicit phone conversations from the Governor."

I laugh. "What?"

She giggles a little of her own silliness. "Tell me what are making you worry? Is it my dad?"

"I have two older brothers, Aryan and Dev," I smile when the camera stays with us.

"Oh the youngest…" Gianna says.

I arch a cheeky eyebrow to her. "What's wrong with that?"

She chuckles, and is ready to say something when our waiter comes with the wine we had ordered. One of my favourite Chardonnays.

The camera only sticks around while we are joking about the wine, once we are served it moves on to the next table.

"Your dad isn't something I have forgotten about but…I'm worried about you."

Gianna looks at me in confusion, a tiny little crease forms in her forehead and she looks at me for a long moment, but before we are able to go further with it, the producer, Kelly, comes to our table.

"How you guys are doing?" she says with a smile.

It takes a second or two to Gianna snap out of her frown, but by the third second the big smile takes over her face. I would almost believe it is natural if isn't for the corners of her mouth quivering.

"We are going to keep it like this for a few minutes more until the food arrives," she explains. "Then we are going to have the camera with you while you eat."

"The whole meal?" Gianna asks.

"No, no, just enough to get something of your first date. Do you know what you guys want to talk about?"

"I thought this was supposed to be natural?"

"Sure, sure," Kelly waves me away. "It's just good for you to have the conversation flowing so you don't get stuck when we are on you."

"Some dates have long periods of silence," Gianna says, but she's smiling, we both know she's only messing.

"I know, Gigi, I've been in plenty of those." With a wink, she moves away.

I'm watching the producer approach a new table when Gianna says, "Why would you be worried about me?"

I shake my head. "We can talk later. Half-twelve?" I send a little smile her way, but she isn't amused.

"Nadia, why are you worried about me?"

"Because… I don't know where you stand with all of this. Have you ever dated a woman?"

In the moment it's out of my lips I know it's a mistake, Gianna purses her lips thin and sighs.

"I'm not judging… I'm just wondering…"

"This isn't the case, though. This experiment was for people who believed it was possible to date regardless the appearances. Gender included."

"I know, I know… But the idea is different of when it actually happens, isn't it? You were open to the possibility, but now it's real. I am here."

"So am I," sipping on her wine.

"Is it so bad that I'm wondering where you stand? I would have asked you but…" I look around and I hope she understand my meaning, we barely have time off cameras.

"You could've asked last night."

She's right, I nod and I can't say much more than that.

"You think I'm going to lead you on?"

"No!" I say straight away, "I'm just…"

She waits patiently but I'm lost for words. I have no idea what I am worried about. I should be worried about the whole career aspect of things, but instead I'm overthinking about whether the pretty girl likes me or not.

I shake my head feeling small. "I guess I was just insecure."

Gianna frowns and pushes her bottom lip out, it's like she's sorry for how pathetic I've turned to be in the last couple of sentences.

"It's a little offensive."

I nod, and sip of my wine. "I guess you're right."

She sighs. "I never dated a woman," she says slowly, "But I thought you were very pretty when we met."

I'm a serious woman, I should do better but my smile grows when she admits it.

"Don't be so pleased with yourself."

"I thought you were absolutely gorgeous."

Gianna's cheeks turn red straight away. She makes a funny squeaky sound that is right between a hiccup and a whistle.

Gianna cleans her throat. "I never thought..." shaking her head. "I never thought much of it. So yes, if we weren't in this together maybe I would never ask you out. But things worked out, didn't they?"

I nod, they did work out in a way I wasn't expecting, but it doesn't change the feeling right in my gut. "So you're telling me you won't have a problem telling your family and friends?"

"I expect it to be as awkward as if I was dating anyone else from the hospital," she says matter-of-factly. "It's about the fact that you're the head physician and nothing else."

I look at her for a second because I want confirmation. I

want to know she's really open to this, whatever this might be. When Gianna looks up, I see the fire on her eyes, the certainty, and the only thing I can do is nod my head and accept that I have to trust her.

I breathe deeply and chuckle. "Sorry, it got a little intense there."

To my surprise, she smiles, "Where's a good Buzzfeed quiz when we need it?"

"Have you wondered if that's the whole magic under this kind of thing?" I ask. "The intensity of it all," I shrug. "It does feel rather dramatic..."

"I guess when you know what you want, you expect nothing less of your supposed partner," she tells me. "We were supposed to ask the hard questions."

"All the time?"

She shrugs. "Might as well."

I think she's funny and I'm ready to start on the hard conversation just to test her theory, but that's when food arrives, and Kelly is just right with it.

I close my mouth and give a closed lipped smile to Gianna. We should have talked about what to say in front of the cameras after all, because when they are on me, I am lost for words.

"Come on, don't be a wimp!"

Gianna opens her door straight away with a frown, "I'm not a wimp!"

"Let's go…" I whisper and pad my way through the corridor of the third floor.

"I didn't show you this way so you could use it every day you know?" She's whispering-yelling behind me.

I turn around and smile, I walk backwards for a second. "It's going to be fun, let's go!"

She can't stop her wide smile. I'm trying my best to make up for this afternoon. I knew it, from the moment I was back in my room and got in the shower, that I had let the emotions take the best of me. When they weren't even real emotions. No, they were clearly fabricated by the isolation and the intensity of the program.

Dating was supposed to be fun. We were supposed to be getting to know each other. It is clear, if I want a chance with

Gianna, I need to let us to be light.

When I turn around to go down the stairs, she rushes to keep up with me. I'm only down two steps when she takes my hand, "Wait for me!"

I look at her over my shoulder, "You know the way…"

"I don't want to be caught alone!"

"I bet that's a better option than being caught together…"

"Why?"

I stop in my tracks and I turn around, she's just a step behind me, taller than me for just an inch. I see her dry swallow by our proximity. I can count the freckles on the bridge of her nose.

"Nadia," she whispers. I do nothing. I just stand there waiting.

Gianna's hands travel from my hands to my arms and they rest there. She watches their movement for a second, and then she looks up at me again with a timid smile. It's always directed at me.

"I always thought you didn't like me very much," I say to her. "You always had the biggest of smiles for everyone but to me…"

She bites her lip. I watch while she does it.

"I wasn't sure about you in the beginning, but…"

"I wasn't sure about you too," I confess.

"Why?" she asks taking a little step back, but I follow her.

"Because you were walking around and everyone in the hospital loves you and…." I shrug. "I wanted to make a good impression with the staff."

She smiles a little. "You did. They like you." And Gianna adds, "They would be very vocal if they didn't."

"To me?"

She giggles, "To me. Plus, Maria messes around with you, she's the hardest of the lot."

I smile too, it's that simple. I shake my head and step away. "Come on, I have a surprise for you…"

I go down a few steps and she's right on my heels, "A surprise? What do you mean?"

"Wouldn't be a surprise if I just told you, right?" I keep going downstairs.

"Nadia, what the hell are we doing…"

I glance back to her arch my brown. "I have never heard you curse."

"I'm a McKenna," she whispers on the automatic.

We are close to the bottom steps when I turn once more. "Why are you a volunteer?"

I know I catch her by surprise, the frown tells me so, I ask again, "You know everything, you could have a job…"

"I'm a nurse," she tells me all of a sudden. "I went to school, and I graduated."

That is completely news to me. "What… I… Who knows that?"

She shrugs. "Maria." Of course. "Her boyfriend Xavier. My friend Rina and my brother Dennis."

I'm lost for words, but when you think about it, it makes complete sense. I caught the nurses asking for her opinion once or twice, I just assumed some people didn't know she was just a volunteer.

"Why the secrecy?"

"My mother would never let me be a nurse. She wouldn't be convinced even if I wanted to go to med school, but no offense I'm at the hospital for too long to know I would prefer to be a nurse. Dennis helped me to hide it from her." Something shines on her face, "He thinks I can be a good nurse."

I take her upper arms in my hands. "You're already a brilliant nurse, Gianna."

She blushes, "Thank you."

"Ok, let's try again, Nurse McKenna, why aren't you being paid like one?"

"Because it's easier for my mother to think I'm just a volunteer. She doesn't want me to work."

I look right into those huge blue eyes and something starts to form the puzzle of Gianna McKenna. I don't want to ask her once more about us, I don't want to go there after deciding today was to be a light day. However, I can't stop wondering why would she let her mother control so much of her life.

"Stop thinking about this," she tells me. "It's our secret ok?"

She offers me her pinkie finger and I smile and take it. Her hand is warm and nice, like the rest of her. I stop myself from going for a kiss, it's like something tells me it isn't the right time.

Gianna has no such voices whispering in her ear; she leans over and kiss me on the lips.

I stay still for just a second, as she lights up the tip of my toes to the last strand of my hair. I feel my skin tingle when I capture her bottom lip with both of mine. Gianna comes closer, her hands falling on my hips as I slide my hand from her cheek to the back of her neck.

It's the best kiss I've ever had.

I have no words, neither am I'm interested in them anymore. When she lightly bites me, I'm sure I whimper, and that's when it stops.

Gianna stops kissing me suddenly and steps a half of an inch away, "Did you hear that?" she whispers.

"What?" I reply confused.

This time I hear it perfectly, the distinctive steps coming down the stairs where we are. I take her hand and pull her arm, "Come on!" I mouth, but she looks terrified. I pull her arm again and she finally moves.

We go down as quickly and silent as possible, when we reach

outside, I breathe again.

I look to my side and she's laughing, and I tell her, "You were scared as well!"

"I know…" another giggle. "But you are very composed everyday…"

I shake my head and pull her by the hand. She follows me without question. We keep stealing glances at each other. I still feel her lips on mine; they're right there, like the most wonderful ghost.

I bring her around the glass house like she had done to me. I know we don't need to anymore, but we keep padding our way around.

I know I had done good when I hear the gasp coming from her. Because right when we turn left from the glass house, in the same steps we once were, waiting for us are Jeff, Natalie, Josh and Trevor. Josh shows her the wine bottle on his lap and we all giggle.

Gianna shakes her head in disbelief and gasps again just once more when she sees the last person there: Shay Bernard.

Looking from Shay to me, Gianna opens a huge smile. Unexpectedly, she hoists me by the waist, hugging the life out of my mid-section. I chuckle and she kisses my neck. "Thank you."

"You're welcome, Gigi."

She beams at me for a second, and then hops to shake Shay's hand.

"This is perfect."

Shay looks around at the three couples she put together and shakes her head in disbelief.

"Don't be so surprised it works," I tell her.

Shay makes a face to me. Josh just passed plastic cups with wine along to all of us. Shay sips from her wine and smiles once more. "I know the matching would work if people were open enough, but we depended on people being open."

"We know a few couples gave up in the middle," whispers Natalie. "I thought it was so sad."

Shay doesn't think is sad though, I can see it on her face. "There was a colleague once that wanted to stop smoking. He complained everyday about the habit, said it ruined many family holidays. He was always in a bad mood when out of cigarettes for too long, you know?" We all followed her story in silence. "So another friend in common showed him this book that everyone swears by and he insisted for my colleague to try it. A year goes by, I meet him again and he's still smoking so I assume the book wasn't a sure thing. He says he never read it. I then say, I know sounds like a bunch of shit you know? But you never know, it might work…" Shay shakes her head and smiles at us. "Then he tells me he's sure it will work. That's why he never read it."

Shay chuckles while we all raise our eyebrows. "It's a silly example, you know. What I'm saying is that I knew it wouldn't matter how perfect our matching calculations were, if the people weren't ready for it, we would end up with no couples at all."

I look at Gianna and she's eating up Shay's words like she's the Messiah. I try not to call attention to it, I don't want her to feel embarrassed, but she catches me and bumps her shoulder to mine. "Stop!" Gianna whispers to me.

"I'm not doing anything!"

"Let me do some fan-girling."

"It's alright…" I laugh away.

People are talking all around us, as I think the other two couples are also very interested in getting to know Shay and even asking a few questions about the matching. She tries her best in answering diplomatically.

I'm happy I called them over. It was a last-minute decision. I just wanted to give Gianna something and giving her Shay was the best I could come up with. However, the two couples were an after-thought, one that I was glad to have had.

After our second bottle of wine is open, Gianna fills our

glasses and then holds me by my waist once more, hugging me. I smile and embrace her with my free hand.

"This is amazing," she whispers.

"I'm sorry for this afternoon," I tell her.

She brings her head up and looks directly at me, frowning that very confused frown.. Shaking her head she adds, "Don't be sorry. I understand why you were asking. I didn't like it, but I understand."

"It's all so intense," I say, doing my best not to be overheard. "Sometimes it feels like we have to figure out everything straight away…"

Gianna comes even closer, her left hand digs into my waist holding me in place. "We don't need to figure out everything straight away. But I promise I will." She smiles, that easy way that makes everyone believe in fairy tales.

Her forehead meets mine, our breath mixing. "You believe me when I say my dad is not going to mess with your job, right?"

I open my mouth, but no sound comes out. Gianna shakes her head just a little, I feel her hands holding me tighter. "We are in a reality show now," another smile, but this time is different, grows in certainty. "Kelly says we will be the fan favourite, right? If my parents threaten to do anything with you, I tell everyone they are bigots. I will tell the word John McKenna is trying to keep the best couple from *Dating Blind* apart."

I chuckle, I know she's being silly. Gianna can't possibly be serious about this. Not the girl who just confessed me she doesn't have the job of her dreams because of her parents.

"It will never come to this," I tell her, "I will talk to a lawyer and…"

"Uh…" she squeezes me once more, "Talk to Darren!"

"Who's Darren?"

"He's the solicitor who took Dr Abram down. The board is already afraid of him anyways."

I laugh and nod. "Alright, I'll talk to him. See it's all going to be fine."

She's inches away from me for a second, just so we can look at each other's faces. "I know, I'm trying to convince you about that!"

I shake my head and bring her back. "And I am promising you," she opens her mouth to argue, but I take her mouth and kiss her hard.

Melanie Steward: *"Welcome to Dating Blind Reunion!"*

The crowd is on their feet applauding nonstop. It's the first live show of Dating Blind, and Melanie is clearly enjoying it.

"It's been a great season, don't you think?" she asks and the crowd whistles. Clapping hands are all she needs for an answer.

"It has been an entire year since the participants were on the show, and we are dying to know how are final couples are, so please give your warmest welcome to... Josh and Trevor!"

The crowd is standing once more. A few banners go up with Josh and Trevor's names and glitter hearts all around it. They enter the stage with big smiles. Josh had grown a beard and Trevor had grown hair and is now blond. Besides that, they look the same as a year ago when they show was filmed. Maybe a little happier. Trevor takes a seat just beside Josh's wheelchair.

"Natalie and Jeff!" calls Melanie and once more the audience claps.

Different banners come up. People jump up and down when Jeff and Natalie arrive holding hands. Jeff is only smiles. He takes Natalie's left hand and shows the audience, they go ballistic on the sight of the big engagement ring.

"Oh wow!" Melanie is saying when Jeff and Natalie sit down beside Josh and Trevor.

"And of course... Are you ready?" Melanie sets the crowd on fire. They're all jumping up and down, many banners up now, red and purple letters decorate their names.

"The absolute fan favourites and the country's best couple, welcome, Gianna and Nadia!"

It's impossible to hear anything when they step on the set. People screaming, so many lights shining. It is hard to understand what's happening and what people are saying.

Melanie applauds as well, with a big smile on her face she watches as Gianna and Nadia sit with the rest of the cast.

Little by little, the audience quiets down and Melanie finds a seat just on the side of everyone.

"How's everyone today?" She wants to know.

A round murmur of nodding and positive answer.

"Let's start with Jeff, a year since you were in the show. How's been the public's reaction?"

Jeff readjusts himself on the chair and smiles. "It's been great. We thought maybe at first would feel odd to be that open, maybe they would judge us or something. But I think everyone was ready for a show like

Dating Blind."

The audience applauds and Melanie nods. *"Do you think people at home felt connected with your story, Natalie?"*

Natalie nods. *"I said a little about my ex-husband in the first episode. I felt bad but then I got this overwhelming response, so many amazing women who had been through such similar situations like me. There's a world of Natalies out there,"* she jokes and people applaud.

"That's amazing. You have a non-profit organization now, am I correct?"

Natalie nods. *"It's hard for some people to ask for help from the police, and take the necessary steps to ensure their own safety. At It Could Be You, we help with no questions asked."*

Applause follows, on the screen the contact to Natalie's organization comes on in neon blue and pink letters.

"Now, Josh and Trevor, how was this year for you?" Melanie asks.

"Intense," chuckles Josh.

"Did you imagine you would be one of only three couples who survived all the dates?"

Josh chuckles and looks at Trevor. Trevor answers, *"Anyone who knows Josh wouldn't think he would last long. I know his friends now,"* he laughs. *"But the show is more than just a dating show, it opens your eyes to see the possibilities. Even the people who didn't stay in, some of them kept dating and many opened up to different hm..."* he smiles, *"Coupling styles."*

Melanie looks intrigued. *"People we have seen on the show?"*

Josh nods. "Some people felt the pressure of being on TV and maybe dealing with dating someone they would never date before and it's all there, for you to be judged..."

Natalie nods on her chair, Josh looks at her with a tender smile. "It's important to remember the show is a lot for many people. It challenges everything you know about yourself," *Josh explains.* "We talked many times, the six of us, we know we stayed until the end but that doesn't mean the other couples stopped seeing each other or have disproved Dr Bernard's beliefs."

"That's very interesting to hear," *Melanie nods.* "It's good to think some couples are still together. Any names you care to drop?"

The six participants shake their heads together, like it was practiced.

Melanie chuckles. "Alright, I'll forgive you!" *The audience says "aww" but it's in good nature.*

"Now, the couple no one can get enough! How are you Gianna and Nadia?"

People applaud, a couple of whistles sound and Gianna's cheeks turn red.

"We are good, Melanie, thanks," *replies Nadia.*

"How you two feeling? How things are since Dating Blind?"

"Things are good," *Gianna says and she looks to Nadia.* "Right?"

Nadia laughs, she takes Gianna hand and kisses it, while nodding. The audience is in awe.

"You are both still working in the same hospital, right? Nadia is the head physician and Gianna now took a position as a nurse?"

Nadia looks adoringly to her side. "Gianna was promoted to head-nurse. She's fantastic."

"You are the fan favourite, every single person who watched Dating Blind was cheering for you. Did it feel overwhelming at times?"

Gianna nods. "At the start, people would go to the hospital with a broken leg but they wanted us to see them," she giggles.

"It was a weird instant fame," Nadia agrees. "But it was the good type. People liked us, they wanted to see if we were still together."

"That was the most amazing bit," Gianna smiles. "To have so many people telling you how great you are and…It was humbling. We're very grateful."

Melanie nods, she looks around at the six people beside her. "All couples still together?"

They all nod and the audience claps enthusiastically.

"I see Natalie's big rock there…" Melanie says and people cheer.

Natalie blushes. "Jeff proposed when the first episode aired."

Another round of applause.

"They were all involved," she tells the audience, looking at her friends.

"We organised a viewing party at our house," Gianna says, "Jeff told us his plans."

"Other members of the cast and crew were there too," Trevor adds. "We got Natalie's favourite flowers and Sinatra was playing in the *background..."*

The audience goes "uhhh" and everyone laughs.

"Jeff is the master of romance!" Nadia says arching an eyebrow and everyone nods in agreement.

"It was wonderful," Natalie swoons. "He's the best man on earth. And they are definitely the best friends I could wish for."

Everyone cheers, the couples look comfortable with each other. When the camera zooms in on Gianna, she's giggling about something Nadia said to her ear. They look at each other in adoration.

No one knows, but Nadia has a ring in her pocket.

The end.

Visit
amyoliveira.com
The official website of

Amy Oliveira

For more on all Amy Oliveira novels.

Be the first to find out when there's a new book coming, find updates from Amy, downloads, news and videos.

Keep up to date with all the latest news on Amy's books and events by signing in to Amy's official email newsletter.

Join Amy Oliveira at:

@amyoliveira.author @amyoli_author

Printed in Poland
by Amazon Fulfillment
Poland Sp. z o.o., Wrocław
18 April 2021

3a4e5344-9e1d-40ce-b43f-11f4a6438d55R01